The Motherload

A Novel

By

Sarah Lawrence

Printed in Canada

First Printing, 2016

ISBN 978 0 9936637 1 0

For Michael,

You have always believed in me,
even when I didn't believe in myself.

You made me a mother to our amazing boys
and for that I am so grateful.
Thank you and I love you.

For my boys, Nathan, Everett and Jacob,

You inspire me. No one else will ever know the
strength of my love for you. After all, you're
the only ones who know what my heart
sounds like from the inside.

The Motherload

A Novel

Becoming a mother makes you realize you can do almost anything…one-handed

Prologue

I SAT IN my corner office, my view of the city was beautiful. I had wall to wall windows on the 15th floor of our building. In five short years I had gone from graduate school to head writer for *Phanlax* magazine. It covered everything from celebrities and fashion, to technology and current events. It was a smorgasbord of articles and it was popular.

I loved my job and I was dedicated to it. I was single and not being tied down allowed me to be ready in any instant to cover a story. Nights or weekends, it didn't matter. Work was my life and life was good.

***

But as we know, life likes to throw the occasional curveball and the grand universe had different plans for me.

***

On a Monday morning my boss, Henry Stone, called me into his office. He was an older gentleman but still young at heart. He had white hair and little, round glasses. He always dressed in jeans paired with a dress shirt and bowtie. He was his own person and I loved it.

"Hi Evy, how was the weekend?" he asked.

"Really fun, got some great stories and ideas to throw around at our weekly meeting." I answered.

"Good to hear. I'm really happy with how you've been doing. You've been a godsend for this magazine."

This was a great start to a Monday I thought to myself.

"Well, thank you, it's nice to be appreciated and I'm happy you're happy." I replied.

"Here, sit down," he motioned to the chair by his desk, "you're going to need some help. I want you to focus more on just the stories and the experience. I want people to see who you are. I want you to be the face of our magazine for our special interest stories."

I'm pretty sure my jaw dropped and my mouth was wide open. I had to tell myself to shut it, Henry continued talking,

"So, I've hired a photographer to partner with. He'll capture the moments with you, he'll go with you to all your leads, basically he will be with you a good chunk of the day making you a real person to our readers."

I took a moment, "Wow, thank you. This is an amazing opportunity. I'm so honoured that you want me to represent the magazine. When do I get to meet the new guy? Please tell me he's going to be fun to work with…"

And then on cue I heard a voice from behind me say, "I'm not that lame of a guy to hang out with."

I turned around and my jaw literally dropped when I saw who our new photographer was. He was insanely handsome. I looked him up and down, honestly gorgeous. He was tall, darker hair and nice muscles, not too big but you can tell he was strong. His shirt was just tight enough to show them off. His smile revealed dimples. I felt my cheeks go flush. My heart started beating insanely fast and I felt like I was going to pass out. Had I been single too long? I thought to myself.

He held out his hand, "Hi, my name is Mark, I'm looking forward to working with you. I'm a big fan of your writing. I've been following your work. You have a way with words, you keep it real but intriguing."

I smiled. I felt speechless, for a wordsmith like myself this was not normal. Snap out of it I thought to myself. I took a deep, calming breath and shook his hand.

"Nice to meet you Mark, I look forward to working with you."

My boss took over and told me a bit about Mark's background but I wasn't totally listening. I kept sneaking glances over at my handsome new co-worker. I snapped back to attention when they both stood up, shoot I had missed something.

"Evy, can you give Mark a quick tour of the place? Then take him back to your office."

'Oh I'll take him to my office alright...' I thought to myself. I held in a giggle.

"For sure, come on, I'll show you around and then we can go over a game plan for the week in my office."

With that we walked out of my boss's office. I gave him a quick tour and introduced him to a few people along the way. I was walking a lot faster than normal but I really just wanted to talk to him in private. I wanted to know everything about this guy. Finally, we made it to my office.

I closed the door behind us.

"Whoa, nice view," he said as he walked towards the window, "I feel a little intimidated."

I smiled and smelled his scent as he walked by me, he smelled so good. OMG was I seriously smelling him? *Evy, focus.* Before I could get a word out there was a knock at my door. It was my Henry.

"Hey guys, I have Mark's desk and chair headed this way, can you guys make some space in here for it? I want you guys to really get to know each other and work together. Evy, you don't mind sharing do you?"

My office was nice but not huge, throwing another desk in here would make it pretty cozy and I liked being able to hide out with the door closed when I got into a groove writing. Having to share my office just wasn't cool, even though Mark's company would be a nice addition to view, he would be pretty distracting too.

"It's pretty tight in here, do you think there's going to be room?" I asked.

"Sure, just no hanky panky," he winked and walked away leaving the door open.

Did he just say hanky panky? Really? Who says hanky panky. Then as if he was reading my mind Mark whispered,

"Did he say hanky panky?"

I smiled and said, "He sure did, you'll get used to his old-school slang."

Maybe sharing an office wouldn't be that bad.

"Come on, let's do some shuffling and figure out how we're going to cram you in here." I said.

After planning it out the only spot that his desk would fit would be right beside my desk. This was going to be interesting.

***

2 months later

As it turned out, Mark and I worked great together. We had a very similar work ethic and sense of humour. He understood my need for space when I was writing and he used that time to edit photos. He was an amazing photographer. I was blown away with his ability to capture the spirit of the moment.

When we went out on assignments he was great with people. He had a way of engaging with his subjects. We had a lot of fun and it didn't feel like work. The more time I spent with him, the more I was really starting to enjoyed his company too. I realized that I was starting to grow feelings that were more than professional towards him. He made me get those silly butterflies in my stomach. But we worked together and I didn't want to risk the awkward crush on your co-worker thing so I did my best to put those feelings aside.

***

I was finishing up an article at my desk when he popped his head inside the door. I look up, he was so cute I thought to myself.

"So what are you doing this weekend?" he asked.

"I don't really have much planned – What about you?"

"Well, I have a potential date with this girl I've been kind of seeing."

My heart dropped hearing him say that but I played it cool.

"Oh, I didn't think you were seeing anyone, you never mentioned anything."

"Yeah, I wanted to keep things quiet. It's tough to get a read on her. She's really cute though, very sweet, nice, sincere, beautiful. She's been on my mind a lot over the last few months."

I felt so dumb, here I was crushing on this guy and he had been seeing this girl all along.

"Well, she sounds great…good luck, I'm just finishing up this article so…."

"I think you'd like her," he cut me off.

Why wouldn't he stop talking. This was not a conversation I wanted to have.

"Well, if it works out you should bring her by the office one day to say hi."

"That's easy to do, she works in our building…"

Of course she does, how perfect. Now I get to see them be all cutsie-pie together.

"Oh,"

He smiled at me, "Yeah, she's a really cool chick, not quite sure if she digs me though. How would you find out if someone's into you?"

"I don't know, it been awhile since I've had to do that. I guess I would just ask…"

"Ha, no you wouldn't. I know you, you want to be swept off your feet. It's a girl thing. Tell me the truth." He walked over to my desk and sat on it.

I looked at him, straight in his beautiful, blue eyes. He had called my bluff and he knew it. I bit my lip and felt my cheeks go flush. I broke away from the stare and I stood up from my chair, walked to my filing cabinet and started talking while I pretended I was looking for some files.

"Truthfully, if I was into a guy and he thought there might be a chance, I would want him to kiss me. Not a stranger, obviously, but someone who I knew, who I had flirted with and was sending all the right signals to. I would want him to wrap his arms around me and breath me in and kiss me. You can tell so much from a kiss. It really does determine a lot about a person, if they are gentle or aggressive, passionate, warm." I was getting lost in my own fantasy when I turned around and he was standing right behind me.

"So, something like this…"

And he wrapped his arms around me and kissed me with such tenderness that I melted inside. I had butterflies. It felt so good. I got lost in that kiss.

He pulled away for a moment, "I think it's cute that you were getting jealous of yourself."

I punched him in the arm, "Shut up."

And we kissed again and again.

Chapter One

5 years later

I LOOKED IN the bathroom mirror, I had tears rolling down my cheeks. My once styled hair was now thrown up in a messy bun, my perfect make-up was non-existent. I had wrinkles and frown lines. My skin was so blotchy. I lifted my shirt to reveal my stretch-marked stomach that was no longer firm, but jiggled when you touched it. I was a faint memory of who I used to be. I tried to cry as quietly as I could so no one would hear.

I replayed the past 5 years of my life over and over in my mind. It started out like a fairy tale. After a whirlwind romance, Mark and I quickly got engaged and married. We spent a year doing everything newlyweds do, we traveled with work together, we enjoyed each other's company, we bought a house, held dinner parties. Life was perfect. But perfection doesn't last and life decided to throw us a curveball.

We had 3 babies, back to back to back. I had been pregnant for 3 years straight. We knew one day we wanted to have kids but not this soon and not this many, and definitely not this close together. We weren't prepared and it forced us to make some serious decisions in a short period of time. I had finally gotten myself into my dream position at the magazine and I had to give up my job to take care of our growing family. There was no point in paying for childcare for three kids, we would end up paying more than what I would make going to work. It broke my heart to give up that position. I had worked so hard for it and I felt resentful that I was the one that had to give up my dream.

Emotionally, physically, mentally, I had reached my breaking point. I used to want to be needed and now all I wanted was to escape the non-stop neediness that I was constantly attending to. I had three new human beings and their whole world revolved around me. My body was drained from not getting nearly enough vitamins and nutrients as these little beings literally sucked the life out of me. I hadn't had a good night's sleep in 4 years. I was a mess. I was sad and confused.

Mark was barely speaking to me. He too had given up his job as a photographer and took a more secure role at the magazine selling advertising. He hated it but it kept him steady hours and he wouldn't have to travel. He saw me become a zombie of my old self. I tried to explain to him that most days it was hard enough to get out of bed, let alone take care of everyone including myself. He didn't understand and thought I was just being lazy.

We would fight all the time about money, the kids, the house, sex, everything. We were miserable and it was affecting everything.

Our stress levels were so high and then gradually we turned the anger off and just stopped talking to each other. Our answers to each other were abrupt. I was walking on eggshells because I felt as though anything I said was taken out of context and blown out of proportion. So I just stopped talking to him because I was tired of fighting and he did the same.

Here I was, Evelyn James, ready to give up on life. I had been through so much prior to kids, I was tough as balls and so quick-witted, I was a problem-solver and here I was being defeated by motherhood and being a wife. I was so disappointed in myself. I thought that everyone would be better off without me. In this moment I honestly just wanted to die. I was feeling sorry for myself.

Then I thought about what it would be like for my boys to grow up without their mom. I felt guilt because there were parents that were actually sick and dying and would give anything to spend another day with their kids, and I was healthy but wanted to do just the opposite. It was a constant battle in my head.

I heard footsteps coming down the hallway approaching the bathroom door and I immediately wiped the tears away. *Fuck, what was I going to do?*

I heard a little knock at the door.

"Mom?" a tiny little voice said from the other side.

I took a deep breath, "yes sweetie." I replied.

"Can I come in and sit with you?"

I felt a pang of guilt hit my heart. I opened the door and in came my eldest son Luke. He was an old soul, wise beyond his years and had always been so in tune with my emotions. I knew that he knew something was wrong. He came and sat right beside me on the floor.

He grabbed my hand and said, "Mom, I know you're sad, and that makes me sad too. Would a hug make you feel better?"

I wiped the tears from my eyes and replied, "Mom's just having a bad day sweetie, I'll be ok but yes a hug would really help to make things better right now."

He hugged me and squeezed me so tight, I hugged him back hard. My sweet little man.

It was in that moment I realized that I can't allow this to happen again. I can be sad but I can't allow myself to get to this point of no return. I had to find a way to snap out of this and not allow him to see his mom like this again. He was a kid, he shouldn't have to see his mom crying and worrying about me, it should be the other way around. He needed me and so did his brothers. They needed a functioning mom, not an emotional mess. I had to toughen up and stop feeling sorry for myself. I had to take control of the situation. I was the master of my own destiny and I was the only one that could fix the way I was feeling.

I was always a believer that every single thing happens in life for a reason, and it's how we take the hard times determines our future paths.

"Luke, I love you, thank you." I said and I gave him a big kiss. He at that moment had smartened me up and saved my life.

"I love you too mom." he replied.

We hugged again and sat in the bathroom together for a little bit longer. Then the silence was interrupted by a fart.

"Mom, I really have to go poop now." he said.

I burst out laughing. That's something I hadn't done in a really long time and it felt good to laugh. I promised myself that there MUST be more laughter in all of our lives.

I left Luke by himself in the bathroom to poop and went downstairs to find Mark. My eyes were still puffy and red but I didn't care. We needed to talk. The other two kids were in bed already so we could talk uninterrupted.

***

I found him in the kitchen, talking on the phone as usual, he was always on the phone. He saw me approach with my red, puffy eyes and he tried to ignore me and started to walk away. Then without even thinking the words came out of my mouth, "You walk away from me now, me and the boys are walking away for good. Get off the phone, we need to talk." This was for the first time in a long time I wasn't worried about his reaction.

I knew he heard me when he turned around slowly, I waited for him to yell but there was nothing, he said a quick goodbye and hung up.

He was quiet.

I had so many things I wanted to say but now that I had the floor to speak I didn't know where to start. After a short pause, Mark started talking.

"I'm sorry, I know I've been really hard on you lately, this is a really hard adjustment on me. I'm disappointed in myself – I can't think straight lately. I'm miserable and I know I'm taking it out on you and the kids. That's not fair. Everyday when I go to work I wonder to myself…What am I doing? I hate it – I hate going to work, that place is so toxic and then I come home and there is even more chaos. And I feel like I'm arguing with you just trying to prove that I'm right? About what? I don't even know. I'm being a horrible husband."

This was not what I was expecting at all and then he kept talking.

"I know it's not going to be easy, but I do love you and I hope you still love me. I'm holding onto so much anger and resentment towards you because you get to be at home, but I know it's not easy for you, but it's not easy for me either. It's a lot of pressure on me. I hate my job; I miss taking photos."

I could tell he had been holding this all in for such a long time. Here I was thinking he hated me and he was discouraged in himself. I responded back,

"So talk to Henry, the team, they'll let you take photos again, you take beautiful photos. We can figure this out together instead of hate each other and hold resentment towards each other. I want what's best for every single person in this family. That includes you…we can get there but we need to approach this another way because what we're doing, it's not working. And everyone is feeling it. I'm so unhappy I just don't want to say anything because I just don't want to fight. I'm so tired of fighting."

"I know, me too."

"Well if we're both so tired of fighting, why don't we just stop. Let's focus on making this work. We are a team and we need each other."

I took another deep breath and held out my hand and continued talking, "Honestly, you need to do what makes you happy, I know why you stopped taking photos, you did it for us, but the kids are older and I think it's time you went back to what you love, even if you need to travel, we'll be fine. I totally support that. But… I need something too, an outlet, I feel trapped in this house with the kids. I need a project or something to serve a purpose aside from doing laundry, cooking and cleaning. Something to satisfy my soul and reach out to other people outside of this house. I miss writing, engaging with people, helping people."

He reached his hand out and shook it, "Deal, let's make a plan and get our shit together and start having some fun and enjoy life again, and each other." And then he smiled and those dimples came out. That was something I hadn't seen in a very long time, especially directed at me.

He didn't let go of my hand and he pulled me into him and he kissed me. It felt so good and I let out a little groan. It had been so long since he had kissed me with some fire behind it. He ran his hands down my back but the moment was interrupted by the shouts of Luke in the bathroom, "Mom, I got 4 poops out, come check my bum."

I took a moment and I smiled, "to be continued?" I asked.

"Let's put him to bed then I'm putting you into bed." Mark said back.

We looked each other in the eye and smiled. In this moment I knew that it was all going to be ok. It's funny how life can change in such a short amount of time.

Chapter Two

One year Later

I TOOK A deep breath and let my head slip beneath the water. I enjoyed the sound of being under the water and hearing my heart beating, and nothing else. I could feel my lungs starting to burn wanting air in them. Just a few more seconds I told my body but the need for oxygen won out and I resurfaced.

I sat up in the tub and heard the running and screaming of my children down the hallway outside of the bathroom, one was banging on the bathroom door. Then I saw tiny fingers reaching underneath the door. I took another deep breath and went back under the water. This was my twenty minutes of child-free time and I still had a few minutes left before having to go back to the chaos. Even under the water I heard the door crash open. I sat up in the tub again, in came.

"I'm sorry, but…" he couldn't get the words out his mouth before he was pulling his pants down and taking aim at the toilet. He sat down and his ass exploded on the toilet. He left the bathroom door open and in came the boys. I quickly grabbed the shower curtain so they wouldn't see me naked and ask where my penis was. I wasn't in the mood to answer this question again today.

This was the end of my quiet time. Back into mom mode. The smell of poop started to mask the smell of my lavender bath bubbles. I looked at Mark and he started to laugh which just caused tiny farts to come out which made him laugh even harder. The boys of course thought it was hilarious.

"I'm sorry, but it just hit me all of a sudden and this was the closest bathroom." he was still laughing.

I was annoyed and yet trying to hold in my laughter too. As the mom of boys and I had no choice but to find the humour in farts and poop.

"Ok boys, thank you for making sure dad made it to the toilet safely. Can you please go out of the bathroom now and let mom dry herself off?" I said.

They all looked at me and Luke my oldest said, "Mom, what happened to your dinky?"

This caused Mark to start laughing again, which started the fart giggles, which caused a chain reaction of giggles from the boys before they finally left the bathroom.

"Honey, honestly, I'm sorry. I know how much you need some quiet time. It's the tacos we had for dinner…"

I looked at him, "you owe me a bottle of wine." I grabbed my towel and started drying off.

"I'll buy you 2 bottles if you bring me some toilet paper." He responded.

I looked at the empty roll.

"2 bottles of wine and a piece of cheesecake and it's a deal."

"Deal"

I walked out of the bathroom with my towel wrapped around me. There was a line of toys down the hallway and I stepped on a piece of Lego as I walked to the pantry for the toilet paper. The pain of Lego into flesh was the worst feeling. I bit my tongue instead of cursing out loud. F'ing Lego I thought to myself. I grabbed the extra rolls, opened the bathroom door and tossed them at Mark.

"I love you," he said.

I sighed, "I love you too." and I closed the door.

***

We had all come a long way since my breakdown a year ago, and it was all for the better. Stepping down from my role at the magazine to take on the job of being a full-time mom was tough. Even still, I yearned to be a useful commodity of a team, other than my family unit that is.

***

So I started writing again, after all, that's what I went to school for. It wasn't hard to figure out what to write about, since motherhood was all I knew now I began writing about being a mom. I built a small website for all the other moms in the world that were in the same boat as me. Overwhelmed, struggling with life, trying to find a balance and not having a clue where to start. It started as a simple blog for me to document my feelings and journey to getting my life back on track. It quickly picked up a steady stream of followers and I kept getting emails asking me for more advice and my take on situations.

I found a small group of ladies who I knew through various mom groups I was part of and together we built the site into a resource for advice, tips, recipes, cleaning, crafting, organization. If a mom does it, chances are I have an article posted about it. It felt so good to be doing something I enjoyed again. It gave me a purpose and I loved that I was helping other moms out there. Knowing the dark place that I was in, I could understand how important it was to make sure other moms were taken care of too.

***

After Mark was done violating the bathroom we started getting the kids ready for bed. Bedtime was my favourite time of the day. I had kept them alive for another day and finally had a chance to enjoy some downtime with my hubby.

***

Today we both chose to go to bed early, ahhhh married life with kids.

Chapter Three

MORNING ALWAYS seemed to come too soon. I woke up to the banging noise of god only knows what against the wall and a child singing at the top of his lungs. Who needs an alarm clock when you have kids? Then there was the sound of Mark snoring away beside me as he slept through it all. I didn't understand how he didn't hear it. I tried to sneak out of the bed but our dog heard me and he was up and now whining to go pee. And this is how each and everyday of my life started now.

I focused back on getting myself ready and braced myself for the day. I again tried to sneak downstairs to get everyone's breakfast ready before I released them from their rooms but the second I closed our bedroom door, there was my son Luke waiting for me.

"Hi Mom, Ben is being a weirdo – he's going to be in trouble when you see what he did. What's for breakfast?"

"What did your brother do?" I asked as we walked downstairs together to let the dog outside and to make breakfast.

"He got out of his diaper…and he pooped, his room smells really bad."

I looked at him, praying that he was joking, but he was dead serious. I took a deep breath, today was off to a great start.

I continued heading downstairs to the kitchen and focused on making breakfast, a few extra minutes playing in poop wasn't going to do much more damage to my feces covered child.

I opened the freezer and scanned which frozen breakfast would be devoured today. I went with toaster waffles and fresh blueberries. I felt like even though I cheated on the waffle part, the fresh fruit made up for it. I set Luke up for breakfast, put the plates out for the other two and went back upstairs, bracing myself for what would be waiting for me. I could smell the room before I even reached it. It was bad. I walked in and there he was, Ben our middle child, who is three, with shit all over himself, laughing hysterically as he saw me. Then reached his hand out to pass me some – how nice, he wanted to share.

"no thank you, you are disgusting, let's go hose you off." I picked him up, kicked the bedroom door closed, I would deal with that mess later. I carried him straight to the bathroom trying not to barf or let him touch anything along the way, including myself.

I sat him in the tub and started to rinse him off as the tub filled. I gave Ben a fast but thorough bath, trying desperately to get the smell off of him. When I was satisfied that he was clean and no longer had poo residue, I dried him off and threw a new diaper on him. The moment we left the bathroom the youngest, Tom, was now screaming his lungs off. When he was hungry he made sure everyone knew.

I brought Ben back downstairs, strapped him into the highchair, gave him food and then ran upstairs to grab Tom. I wondered to myself how many times a day I actually went up and down these stairs, then part of me just really didn't want to know.

By the time I got back down Luke was finished breakfast so I sent him back up to get dressed, Ben was eating away and I sat down to feed Tom. I knew I would have a few minutes of peace before the next wave of chaos started.

On cue, Ben finished eating the same time Tom did. Luke came downstairs dressed in bright yellow shorts, soccer socks and a dress shirt. I loved this kids style.

He was followed by Mark. He was dressed and ready for work. He had gotten his job back doing photography and he was so happy. The magazine was growing again and he was photographing some very famous people. I was very proud of him. He was just happy to be back behind the camera. He gave his good mornings and goodbyes and out the door he went to work, while I stayed at home with the crew.

***

Today was Monday, which meant it was playgroup day. The local play centre discounted its rate on Monday mornings and almost every mom went there because, let's face it, we're cheap and this was a smoking deal. It was also my "meeting" day with the ladies who helped me manage my website. They have become my ultimate support system and the site wouldn't be where it is today without them.

I packed the day bag – diapers, snacks, toys, a change of clothes for each child and did inventory that I got each child ready too. I took a deep breath and loaded them all into the minivan. Then I said a small prayer that we would make it through the 15-minute drive without crying, yelling or hitting.

I put it in reverse, Tom started crying, Luke reached over and smacked his brother Ben and I yelled at him to stop. Some days I think God really has a huge sense of humour but I also believe he will only give you challenges you can handle – apparently he thinks I can handle a lot.

Once we got moving the kids quieted down and by the time we got to today's play centre, all the tears had stopped and all 3 were quiet. It's moments like these that I treasure – silence was happiness.

Chapter Four

I PULLED INTO the parking lot and circled around 3 times trying to find a spot that was close to the door, that also had room for me to park the mom-mobile aka the mini van. I got so annoyed because so many of the ladies that were there already parked over the line or crooked. A few took up two spots, *"really ladies, this is where the stereotypes of women drivers come from."* I thought to myself. Finally, I found a spot and unloaded my crew and we went inside.

I spotted Chloe. She was, as always, the first one there. I don't know how she did it but she was always on time, she always had her hair done.

Her make-up is on point and her outfit always coordinated.

Not only was she beautiful, she had her masters in economics and was a financial planner in her life before kids. She helped millionaires plan their investments but gave it all up when she had kids. She understood my meltdown more than anyone. She too had to make the switch from the cooperate world to munchkinville. She now worked as a waitress in the evenings so she could spend the days with the kids while her husband worked.

Her attitude was so positive and she was by far my favourite person of our mom group.

"Evy, how are you?" as she came over and squeezed me for a giant hug, "I still can't believe how amazing you look after just having 3 babies back to back. I am so jealous. It's been 3 years since my last baby and I'm still losing the weight. I ordered all of our drinks already."

She had one daughter, Lexi, who was 3 and she was the apple of Chloe's eye. She was the sweetest, most polite child I had ever encountered. She was going to do amazing things when she got older.

"I'm doing good, busy and tired, but good."

She gave hugs and kisses to all the kids, grabbed Tom and smothered him in kisses. He just ate it up. This is one of the many reasons why I love her dearly. She knew how high maintenance he was and knew that I loved passing him off to another set of arms.

With Luke and Ben off playing I sat down to enjoy having my hands free.

A few minutes later came the other 2 ladies of our "clique". Stacey was our granola mom but she was a marketing wizard, she came up with amazing promos, ads and contests. Her mind was always thinking of new things to add to the site and make it better. I couldn't wait to hear what she had in store for this week. The granola mom is the all natural mom, breastfeeds, cloth diapers, all natural organic foods, non-vaccinating, homemade herbs for what ails you, let the kids run free and will eat nothing processed. I totally respect her values but what

I like best is that she doesn't try to push her ways onto you.

Leslie was our helicopter mom. She was the total opposite of a granola mom. She keeps the kids close by, constantly checking them for bumps and bruises, endless trips to the doctor's office and believes every parenting article out there as the truth. Leslie was a computer genius. She built the site, tracked all the visitors, built the keywords and SEO. She got people to come to the site. We are an odd bunch – each so different, but I love them all none the less. Their quirks were what made us such a diverse group and they helped me areas that I didn't know much about.

We got down to business. I had printed out the most recent emails I received and we went through them all to decide which topics seem to be the most popular and what we would write about this week.

Then Stacey piped up,

"I have a new idea, and I think the timing of it couldn't be more perfect. You have the traffic to the site now, so I think you should start branding yourself. Let's start selling items with your logo, catchphrases, let's get the name out there more. You can start with t-shirts, onesies, tote bags. You will be everywhere. I've made some samples already." And she laid out a variety of goodies on the table. They were cute but this was a new direction and more work.

On cue, Chloe asked about pricing for production, retail pricing and she inspected them for quality.

"These are really cute; I think the onesies would be a hit." She said.

"What type of applique did you use? Is it toxic? What type of material are they made from?" Leslie asked.

We all laughed.

"I'm sorry, I just can't help myself." And she laughed at herself.

It was so fun to have this small empire and share it with these ladies. Once business wrapped up and after 2 hours of chit chat and satisfied that the kids are well on their way to being exhausted – mine have the rosiest red cheeks, we say our good-byes and head back home just in time for naptime.

Naptime is my favourite part of the day. Only one child to watch and my chance to do a bit of work, tidy up and take a little break. I threw some cartoons on for Luke and I went to work.

I got settled in to start writing the new articles we had discussed at our meeting earlier today when I heard the front door open and in walked Mark. He never came home during the day so I was instantly worried.

"What's going on?" I asked.

"We need to talk..."

Chapter Five

"I JUST LEFT a meeting and we got offered an exclusive deal to cover and shoot a celebrity wedding feature. We won't know who it is until we arrive. The way they are trying to keep it hush hush it's gotta be big"

Since Mark had gone back to photography with the magazine he was getting a lot of attention and even more exclusive contracts with some very famous people. The reason was first, he was an amazing photographer but second, he treated them like real people, mainly because he didn't follow anything with Hollywood and most times he would do a shoot and not know who the person even was until I took a look at his photos and freaked out over who he had worked with that day.

"That's amazing news." I replied and hugged him.

And then he took a deep breath, "but the catch is the work isn't here in the city, they need me to go on location to Hawaii for 6 weeks for the shoot."

I sat back down. I knew this was going to happen. He used to travel all the time when we worked together and I was surprised that it had taken this long for him to have to leave town for a shoot.

"It's all expenses paid, and the bonus salary is really good, but its 6 weeks away from you and the kids."

I took a deep breath, I couldn't believe I was about to say this, "I can survive 6 weeks alone with the kids, I'll call in some help if needed."

"Are you sure?" he asked

"Yes, this is an amazing opportunity."

He kissed me, "you are the best."

"When do you have to leave?" I asked.

He paused, "my flight is booked to leave tomorrow evening."

"You already have tickets? What if I would have said no…"

He smiled, "Because I know you, and I know how much you have grown this past year and I know you are going to take this challenge to prove it to yourself that you have what it takes to do it on your own. That and I know you'll want me to bring you home a pretty bracelet."

Darn him, he was right on all accounts, especially the bracelet. I loved having something new to wear on my wrist. Especially something authentic from Hawaii.

***

The next 24 hours were spent packing Mark for his trip, stocking up on groceries, household supplies and then I went on a cleaning spree. In my head I was freaking out – how on earth was

I going to do this? I knew deep down I could do it.

"I'll have my phone on me all the time so if you need me for anything just call me ok." He said.

"I know, I'll be ok, we'll miss you." I answered back.

"Are you sure you're going to be ok?"

"We'll be fine, I promise."

He kissed me, he still had a way of giving me butterflies with his kisses. After all these years I still loved him so much.

"Go, have fun, enjoy a bit of freedom, make lots of money, take some great photos, I love you. And bring me back a nice bracelet."

"I love you too, and I might even be really nice and bring back matching earrings for you too."

He walked out the door to the cab waiting and he was off. Time for operation motherload to start.

***

The next day I had called in my reinforcements. Chloe was there first. Followed shortly by the other girls and their kids. The joys of being a mom is that whenever you go anywhere its commonplace that the kids aren't far behind. We set them all up with a movie and we went to the kitchen

"Ok, so what's the plan here? What do you need?" Chloe asked.

"Well, here's the scoop…Mark had the opportunity to take on a 6-week photo shoot in Hawaii. The pay is great but he's gone for 6 weeks. He just left yesterday. I'm going to need some help here and there with the kids so I can keep up with my part of the site. I also really like the idea of selling merchandise, it makes me super excited. Can we handle throwing that into the mix too? Things have been picking up lately and I'd hate to lose momentum now." I said.

Then out of nowhere Chloe burst out crying. We all just stared at her. She was always the one to keep her composure.

"I'm sorry, I'll help you as much as I can but..."she said.

"What's wrong?" Stacey asked

"I've been keeping a secret from you guys and I'm sorry...I was hoping to deal with it but I just heard from the doctors and it's now officially serious. Guys, I have cancer, and it's spreading everywhere rapidly. The doctor gave me a timeframe and it's not very long...." She trailed off.

For a few minutes no one said a word. I was stunned, how could she be keeping this to herself for so long.

Chloe interrupted the silence, "I can't believe all this clean eating, working out and new age crap I believe in and I am full of cancer. For years I didn't put anything bad in my body and this is my reward."

"What can we do?" Leslie asked.

"Keep an eye on Lexi when I'm gone and make sure Adam feels miserable about my death for about a year, then make sure he finds someone to make him happy and that she treats my sweet Lexi like a princess." she answered

"Is there any chance of beating it? Or extending things?" Stacey asked.

"A few months is being optimistic…it could be sooner…."

"Well, shit, anyone else have any totally shitty news to share?" I asked.

Stacey and Leslie shook their heads.

"Ok- so let's make a game plan." I said

We drank wine, talked, cried and figured out how we were going to get through the upcoming weeks and be there for Chloe. I was so thankful to have this amazing group of ladies to call my friends who without a moments hesitation came to not only my rescue but were there for our dear friend Chloe as well during this trying time in her life. What were we going to do without her? I bit my lip and held back more tears. The thought of her not being around broke my heart. I could only imagine what she was feeling.

Chapter Six

I WAS A few days into my stint of being a temporary single mom and I was managing ok. It was busy that's for sure, but I was getting used to things and I kept us on schedule. Mark made a routine of calling before bedtime so he could chat with the kids before bed.

Once we hung up the phone with Mark, the kids went to sleep and my workday began. I sat down and wrote one new parenting article for the site and added how-to article as well. Stacey had added in a few items in a shop section to see what the reaction would be from our fan base. I would get an email notice each time something sold and then set up a production order for Stacey. She had all the supplies at her place and since this was her brainchild we thought it would be best to let her handle the orders for now. Plus, she was the crafty one of the bunch so it just made sense for her to be in charge of this task for now until things got super busy and then we would figure out a game plan for our next step.

Then at the very end of the day I checked all the other emails that came in through the site. I always left this to last because it ensured I would get my work done first before I got side tracked with emails. I could always stop answering emails anytime but the articles were what drove the traffic. My latest ones were focused on surviving life and the kids when your spouse is away. Apparently I was not alone and many moms could relate. The amount of hits and comments had almost tripled since I started posting these particular articles. This meant a lot more feedback to review and a lot more emails to respond to. I felt a little overwhelmed but at least I knew it was temporary and I just had to survive until Mark got back home. At midnight I made a cup of coffee, it was going to be a long night.

***

Over the next few weeks this was how my days were spent. Then came a Wednesday I dreaded. It was my day to take Chloe for her cancer treatment. We were all going to take turns going with her and since this was her first round I really wanted to be there with her. Stacey arrived at my house early to take care of the kids while I would be out.

She smiled at me when she walked into the house. "I brought a bunch of supplies with me, the kids are going to help me while you're out with Chloe."

I loved how she made it sound like Chloe and I were going out together rather than going to sit with her while she had her chemo treatment.

I kissed the kids and was out the door and then I was off to Chloe's house. She didn't live too far away and when I knocked on her door, Leslie answered. She would be watching Chloe's munchkins while their mom was at the doctors.

"Come on in, Chloe is almost ready…." Leslie said. Then in a whispered voice she added, "she's having a rough morning."

She didn't need to say anything else, I understood. Chloe had started having trouble keeping food down lately. I heard the toilet flush in the bathroom and knew that she was most likely vomiting up bile. I felt those damn tears again but I would not let her see me getting emotional.

Chloe walked out of the bathroom with her head held high, "I'm all set, Let's go do this."

Chloe and I rarely had time alone without kids around and as weird as it was to say, it was nice to be able to have time together just me and her.

We checked in at the hospital and waited for a bit before we were brought into the chemo room. As Chloe sat in her chair with needles poking into her arms she asked, "any word from Mark?"

I laughed, "Yes, he's having a wonderful time on the beach. His assignment this week is to shoot the bride and her bridesmaids in bikinis on their yacht. Poor guy…"

She laughed, "yeah, it must be so tough, are you doing ok? Answer me truthfully," she asked.

I looked at her, damn her, she was onto me "I'm exhausted. It is tough, even with the help. I just need more hours in the day. Adding merchandise to the site is exciting but makes me a little nervous. If it's a hit – which I think it will be, it's going to get really busy really fast."

"Is it the family or the site?"

She smiled at me, "Wouldn't it be great if you became a millionaire from this?"

"No me, us, we, I couldn't have done any of this without you girls. We all do our part and we all share in it's successes."

She smiled, "You are such a wonderful soul. Wouldn't it be amazing though?" Then I saw my dear sweet friend had tears building in her eyes, I could see the pain that this made the reality of her situation hit home,

She let one tear fall down her cheek. She didn't wipe it away. My heart ached for her and what she must be feeling. I couldn't imagine. She closed her eyes and took a small snooze, I pulled out my journal and made some sketches for new clothing designs.

***

As I drove her home she asked me an odd question.

"When was the last time you smoked weed?"

I looked over at her completely confused, the van swerved slightly and I quickly corrected it.

That was something I hadn't done in a really long time. In college I dated a guy who sold and smoked quite a bit of it and I hadn't touched the stuff since we broke up. He was also the reason I remained single for so long. Our past was awkward to say the least. He had proposed to me the same day I wanted to break up with him. Talk about not being on the same page. His name was Greg and it was a name I hadn't heard or even thought of in a very long time.

We went to the same college and would often run into each other at mutual gatherings. He never stopped trying to rekindle our relationship all through college. Finally, after graduation, when we went our separate ways, and I hadn't seen or heard from him since.

"Why?" I asked

"Well, I know about the guy you dated in college and I was wondering if…if you still had a way to get a hold of him, I know what he was into when you two were dating and…" she paused then blurted out "I need you to buy some 'green' from him for me. I want to stop this chemo treatment. I've been reading and it helps with the pain and with the nauseous feeling. I'm in a lot of pain and I'm really hungry. I know it's a huge favour but…please…I've talked to my doctor but he isn't willing to write me a medical prescription for it yet. He wants me to wait a bit longer…And you know me, I've always hated putting chemicals in my body, the thought of my hair falling out makes me so sad. I really just want to be comfortable."

I looked over at her, "I honestly have no idea how to get ahold of him, but I may be able to find some for you. Let me do some calling around ok." I already knew in my head who was going to help me with this but I didn't want Chloe know. She smiled and said thank you and then fell asleep again.

After I dropped Chloe off at home I sent a text message to Mark and asked him to call me.

A few minutes later my phone rang and I talked to him through the Bluetooth in the van as I drove home.

"What's up dollface?" Mark asked.

"Do you still have your contact for the *'weedman?'* Chloe is asking, she is choosing comfort over chemicals and I want to be able to help her. Her doctor isn't willing to write a prescription for her right now." Mark had so many contacts and I knew that he would be able to get in touch with someone who could help me out. I'm always leery of letting people know just how many contacts he has.

Mark started laughing, "Man, there is never a dull moment. I know someone who can hook her up. Let me do some calling around and I'll arrange it ok."

I smiled, he didn't even hesitate, "thank you for doing this."

"Don't thank me yet, I'll shoot you a text when I have it all organized ok."

"Sounds good, love you honey."

"Love you too."

We hung up just as I was pulling into my driveway. I couldn't wait to see what Stacey had accomplished today. I turned the van off and my phone buzzed. It was a text from Mark:

ALL IS GOOD. HE'LL COME BY THE HOUSE AT 8:30 TONIGHT. NAME IS JOHN. IT'LL COST $50. THIS GUY IS LEGIT.

I replied back:

THANK YOU. I OWE YOU XOXO

And of course he had to get the last word in:

YES YOU DO, I'LL SAVE THAT FAVOUR FOR WHEN I'M BACK.

And he included some choice emojis that made me laugh. When I walked into the house I was greeted by Luke jumping at me and asking,

"Guess what I ate today mom?"

"What sweetie?" I asked. Knowing Stacey it would be something very organic and new to him.

"Dumbass" he said with such conviction.

I was taken aback by his answer, "pardon me?"

"Dumbass, it's made of chicken pee. It sounds really gross but it tasted yummy."

It took me a moment and then I realized that he was taking about hummus and chick peas. At that moment I knew I had a new blog article. I loved inspiration like this. I kissed him on the forehead and we chatted more about what he did that day. Apparently Stacey ran a sweat shop while I was gone since. She put all the kids to work "helping" cut vinyl, sort clothing sizes and colours. She was a genius. She got a lot done. I was amazed. She had close to 50 shirts and onesies ready to be added to the shop.

"I took photos too and I have a list of sizes and colours available. When Mark is back we need him to take better pictures of us modelling them. It will have more of an impact and let's be honest. His camera is a bit better quality than my smartphone. If it gets busier I'm going to start needing some serious grown-up help. Everything is posted and active in the shop. Let's see what happens." She hugged me and was off and running with her kids.

I ate supper with the boys, I was lazy and ordered a pizza. Then we just chilled on the couch and watched a movie. It felt good to just hang out with them. Things had been so busy this last little bit it was nice to slow down and enjoy some time with them. It was getting close to bedtime and Mark called for his daily check-in time with the boys. I answered the phone

"Hi sweetie, Man I miss you guys, mostly you though...not so much the kids." He laughed, "nah I miss them too, who would have thought that."

"I miss you too, thank you for setting things up for Chloe. So who is this guy that's going to come by? I haven't dealt with anything like this in a long time. Pardon the pun."

"It'll be fine, just keep to small talk, he knows it's not for you. It'll be about 5 minutes. In and out. He'll have everything sorted out for you."

"I didn't think I would be doing this today that's for sure. What about you? What did you do today?"

"I never thought I'd say this but I am surrounded by these beautiful women, snapping photos of them in bikinis and they are driving me crazy. These girls don't have a brain in their heads. YOU, have spoiled me for other women."

"I would hope so."

"How's business?"

"Business is really good actually. I've been getting a lot of new followers, thank you for leaving me here, the new articles about surviving alone are extremely popular and we've started selling some merchandise through the site too. Some fun t-shirts and baby clothes, we're going to see what happens, oh…we also need you to take some photos of us modelling our fashion line when you're back ok?"

"Really? Good for you. I'm so proud of you honey. I'd be happy to do that for you ladies, I think that's a great idea. How are you managing things?"

"I'm really tired. The girls have been great helping out but they have their families too." And then it happened. All those tears I had been holding back decided to come out and I cried and cried. "I'm sorry, I'm just sad about Chloe, and the kids are being their normal selves but I feel like I'm neglecting them because I'm staying up late with the site. I feel like I'm running on empty and I need to sleep, I'm so tired, you know how I get with no sleep. And I really need a hug."

There was a moment of silence, "Do you want me to come home?" he asked, "say the word and I'm there."

I really did want him home so badly, but we were 2 weeks in and I knew that in reality I just had to suck it up.

"I want you home but stay there. I miss you but I will handle it. It's hard and I just need to have my breakdown and then I will regroup and it will be fine."

"You are so amazing; did I tell you that today? I am so proud of you."

That was exactly what I needed to hear, "thank you…"

"You got this honey, you can do it, I believe in you. I love you."

"I love you too."

I looked at the clock and realized it was already the kid's bedtime.

"Can I talk with Luke for a few minutes before he goes to bed?"

I called Luke over and he clicked to facetime with Mark. Luke gave him details on all of his latest activities. He grabbed the phone and walked around the house showing Mark all of the stuff he was missing since he was away.

"And here's the pile of laundry mom still has to clean, and here are the dirty dishes, and most days we get happy meals for lunch and for supper but today we had pizza."

Damn you Luke, you are selling me out right now.

"Today Dad, I ate chicken pee dumbass. Dad, I miss you."

"I miss you too buddy, can you give me a hug and kiss through the phone?"

"No, I can't reach through the phone dad..."

"Can you pretend?"

"Sure." And he gave a giant fake hug and kiss to his dad.

Then in a whispered voice he said, "Luke, can you give mom a big hug and kiss for me too. And tell her she's doing a good job?"

"Ok," Luke came over and squeezed me tight and gave me a big kiss. "That's from dad, not from me" he said and then passed me the phone back.

I looked at Mark over facetime, he was smiling, "Looks like Luke gave up your secrets, 2 happy meals in one day?"

"Yup, desperate times call for desperate measures."

"I guess only 2 times today isn't too bad. If it was me, it might be 3. And chicken pee…"

"Chick peas, hummus."

Mark burst out laughing, "man I love that kid, let me know how things go with your 'dealer' ok."

"I will, I love you."

"Love you too."

We signed off. I wished he was here.

Chapter Seven

As I WAS putting the kids into bed my anxiety was growing with each passing minute. I disliked the idea of a drug dealer coming into the house, especially someone I didn't know, but I trusted Mark and like he said it would only take a few minutes. This was for Chloe and I kept reminding myself of it.

I tucked Luke into bed and kissed him goodnight. Repeated with Ben and then one last time with Tom. I closed his door and a few moments later the doorbell rang.

My heart jumped out of my chest. I took a few deep breaths and slowed my breathing down.

I opened the door and there he was, Greg, my ex, was standing at my door. I don't know who was more surprised. Clearly he had no idea I would be his customer.

We stood there for a few moments. We looked at each other. It had been so long since we've seen each other I felt the need to simply look at him. It seemed so surreal. I think he felt the same.

After a few minutes of us staring at each other I said,

"Hi"

And replied. "Hi"

Then I realized that neither one of us had said anything beyond hi.

"Um, are you here why I think you're here, I was expecting someone named John…"

"Yeah, he's my employee, he bailed, and my contact said this was a big deal so I came instead…I was not expecting to see you here…"

Then another few seconds of awkward silence and I said,

"Would you like to come in, thank you for coming here."

He smiled and walked into the house and it just felt so weird to have him come into my world. It was past and present crashing together.

He looked at the pile of boxes full of clothes that Stacey had completed during the day, "looks like you're busy."

"Yeah, it's from my website I run."

"I know, I read it, well I should say all the ladies I know read it and they talk about you a lot so I check it out from time to time. You've really done well with your writing. I remember a time when you wanted to interview celebrities and cover major events. Quite a switch to writing the world of parenting."

I felt a pang of hurt with that comment,

"Well, my life had changed since we've been together. It's not exactly how I pictured it but I wouldn't change it for the world."

He stopped at the kitchen table and laid out his scale and opened up his backpack full of pre-measured, shrink wrapped goodies.

"I didn't mean to be disrespectful, it's just like you said, things are different and our paths in life took us in different directions." He pulled out a few baggies and put them on his scale. "I picked out a few different strains for you...I'm sorry..."

"Oh, it's not for me, it's a friend of mine. She has cancer." I interrupted him.

He seemed to relax a bit,

"I thought it was for you, I'm glad you're ok, but...I'm sorry to hear it's your friend..." he paused, "I made some notes on the bags, the name and what the impact will be, so depending on the type of day she's having, she can choose what suits her best."

I was shocked at his thoughtfulness, "thank you, that's really nice of you..."

"Well, there are quite a few patients I 'deal' with and these are their preferred choices."

"Oh, I see," I was feeling so awkward right now.

"What do I owe you for everything?" I asked as I gestured to the stuff on the scale.

"Nothing, this round is on the house. Think of it as a peace offering for my stupidity oh so many years ago." He seemed humbled by his words.

"No, please, let me give you something, you came all the way here."

"Honestly, it's fine, a belated wedding gift to you."

I smiled, I knew I was not going to win. "Well, thank you." There was another moment of silence.

"Can I ask you a question?" he asked.

My heart skipped a few beats, I knew I couldn't escape what was coming next and I nodded my head yes.

"Why did you call it quits? Truthfully." He asked.

I knew that I couldn't sugar coat the answer so I was nothing but truthful, "Aside from you being a drug dealer, and not telling me but rather me getting to find out, I didn't feel like I could move forward in life with you. I really did care for you but I knew if we stayed together I would still be in the same spot. That I would be happy but not fulfilled."

He cut me off, "And are your fulfilled? Are you living the life of your dreams?"

I smiled, "Yes, it's better than what I could have dreamed of. Life threw a lot on my plate and there was a moment when I didn't know what I was going to do, but I made it through stronger than when I went in."

"I'm glad to hear you're happy. I've been wanting to say this for a long time now, but I'm sorry that I made your life hell after we broke up. I was devastated. I wasn't expecting it and…I was ready to move forward in life with you. I had bought a ring for you. I asked you to marry me, so when you sprang the break up on me instead, I didn't understand…"

My stomach flip-flopped, we had never fully talked about the end of our relationship but this moment brought back a lot of memories and feelings.

"I still do have that ring too, not in a weird stalker way but I was too embarrassed to return it and I didn't know what to do with it. So I still have it in my sock drawer at home. I really don't know what to do with it. I guess I should have sold it."

I felt terrible, but I was thankful that I ended things when I did.

"You should sell it, use it to invest in something, let it make you some money." I looked at him and felt sorry for him. All those years he had kept this reminder of a failed relationship in his sock drawer. Every time he went in there it would be sitting there looking at him.

"I wouldn't know what to invest in, green is my only thing for so many years that I took the time to learn about.I feel like it needs to be used to change someone's life. It was meant to change yours…I dunno, nevermind, forget I even said it. I have simply wasted my time on earth so far."

"You haven't wasted your life, you're a late bloomer that's all. And I'm sorry, you truly are a good person"

He laughed, "I know, I just don't make the best decisions right?"

I looked at him, "It's never too late to start making good decisions."

He smiled again, "you are such a mom now. I better get going, Don't worry about me, I'll be fine.I have a bunch of people in your neighbourhood to visit. If you need any more, give me a call, thanks for the talk."

"You're welcome, and thank you."

He headed out the door and I watched him walk towards his car, then he turned and walked back to the house.

"Did you forget something?" I asked.

"Yes…" and out of nowhere he kissed me. It caught me off guard and I pushed him away. "I'm sorry, but I couldn't just leave. I messed up and if I could I would do it all so differently. Mark is a lucky guy." And that was it, he turned and walked away. I stood there stunned. What an end to the day.

I opted to send Mark a text instead of calling

HE CAME, HE DELIVERED, HE'S GONE. DOOR IS LOCKED. SWEET DREAMS XOXO

I chose to leave out the details. I would tell Mark about what happened. But I honestly did not want to do it today. My emotions were on too much of a rollercoaster ride today.

Then I looked at the giant pile of boxes and was reminded that I still had work to do. I sat down at the computer and started to write. Today I had a lot to talk about.

***

When I finally crawled into bed it was close to 2a.m. I knew the morning would come too quick and before I let myself fall asleep I promised myself that the next day would belong to the kids. It was going to be a fun day with mom and I was going to do no work, no drama, just fun with them. Everything else would have to wait.

Chapter Eight

WHEN I WOKE in the morning the house was quiet. I had a moment of sheer panic. Why was it quiet? Then I looked at the clock. 8am. I looked at all the kid's cameras we have in their rooms that we can access through out phones. I couldn't believe it. They were all still sleeping. Did I dare go back to sleep? Before I gave my mind a chance to think about it I closed my eyes and slept for another hour before Luke crawled into my bed to say good morning. It was going to be a good day.

I sent a quick message to Mark letting him know that I was having a date with the boys but I needed to talk to him later. Outings with the three boys was tricky trying to plan it around feeding and napping schedules so I thought an adventure walk would be fun. I could push the little guys in the stroller, Lance could enjoy a walk and Luke would be in charge of finding "specimens" as we went along.

The weather was beautiful and as we all walked along we spotted all kinds of wildlife, collected lots of rocks and sticks. We found a spot by the river to have a picnic. It was perfect. This would be one of those days that I would keep in the mom rolodex. It felt good to take a day off. I snapped some pictures and when Luke started slowing down on the walk I knew it was time to head back home.

We had a simple supper, homemade, not from a drive-thru. The beautiful part of days spent outside is that the boys are exhausted when we get home and it's an early night. I tucked them all into bed and sat down on the couch.

I called Mark, I needed to tell him about what happened last night. He listened while I explained in great detail everything that happened, even this kiss.

"Ugh, I am so disappointed in myself, I should have just slammed the door in his face. I'm so sorry..."

"Evy, I'm sorry, I sent him there, I had no idea he would be the one that would show up. This is my fault. I know you and you didn't lead him on, and it was a kiss initiated by him and you stopped it in its tracks. I'm proud of you, really. I'm not mad."

I felt relief that he understood. We talked a bit longer and then we said goodnight. I kept yawning, the fresh air had gotten to me too. I was so tempted to close my eyes and go to sleep too, but I had to take advantage of the extra time I had to get some work done.

I wrote my article for the day which was about taking the time to slow down, unplug and enjoy the innocence of being a child. Not having a schedule and simply letting them enjoy doing – letting them be the leaders on the adventure.

Then I checked the order emails, I hadn't looked all day so when I filtered through I thought there must be something wrong, we had over 200 orders. How was this even possible? I double-checked everything and each was a different order. I couldn't believe it. I did the math quickly in my head of our profits multiplies by 200. I highlighted them all, saved them and sent them to Stacey, she was going to freak out in the morning. I laughed to myself. I knew that tomorrow we would be busy but as for today my work was done. I might actually get to bed early today. It was only 11:00pm. I had the choice of going to be right now...it would be the first time in bed before midnight in a very long time. In fact, I couldn't even remember the last time I was in bed before midnight. Or, now that the order emails were done I could check the correspondence emails. I hadn't done it all day either and I knew if I left it for tomorrow there would be a lot more to deal with and tomorrow was already shaping up to be a busy day.

I set the timer on my phone for 30 minutes. I decided to filter through the emails, delete the junk first off, then I sorted comments and messages into another folder. Then I filtered through the remaining few emails. Once all this was done I looked at my timer and I had 2:45min left. I gave the remaining emails a quick scan, one caught my eye. The subject line read "Mom's keeping it real – interview." The sender was D. Parker. I flagged it to read tomorrow morning. I was tempted to open it, very tempted, but I knew if I read it that I wouldn't be able to sleep tonight and right now that was more important than anything.

I was excited to go to bed early. I was almost giddy. I brushed my teeth and quickly undressed and put on my comfiest jammies. I crawled under the blankets and sprawled out on the bed. Today it felt extra comfy. I closed my eyes and fell into a blissful sleep.

I dreamt about the day with the boys, walking in the trees and soaking our feet in the river. Then little fishies nibbled on our toes. Then a bunch of fish started nibbling on them…I woke up and kicked my feet so hard trying to shake off the feel of fish nibbles.

I rolled over in the bed and tried to get back to sleep and then I felt a tickle on my forehead. I swatted it away with my hand. I felt it again and I again swatted it away. I heard a small snicker and I muttered, "go back to bed you turd." Thinking that it was Luke playing a joke on mom.

"I'd like to go to bed but it seems you've gotten used to taking over the whole bed, so if you'd kindly move over then I'll let you go back to sleep."

It took a few moments for my sleepy mind to realize that the voice belonged to Mark and he was home and he was here. Right now.

"Are you really here?" I asked.

"Yes, move over." He pushed me over and gave me a giant squeeze, followed by a huge kiss. "Ugh, your breath smells like ass."

"You're an ass," I replied quickly, "are you seriously here? Why are you here, tell me in the morning ok…"? I was already falling back asleep.

"I love you, have a good sleep." He said as he gave me one last squeeze, her knew how important sleep was to me.

It didn't take long to drift back to dreamland but it felt nice to feel the warmth of his body next to me again.

Chapter Nine

WHEN I WOKE up in the morning I felt so refreshed. I rolled to the side and was stopped by a giant lump in the bed. It took me a moment to remember that last night wasn't a dream and Mark really was home.

I smiled and curled up to him. I took a deep breath and took in his scent. As I pulled him closer to me he woke slightly and grabbed my hand pulled it over his body. We snuggled for a few minutes and then he rolled over.

He didn't say a word, he kissed me. It felt so good. I soaked it up. It brought me back to when we first began dating and how he could awaken places in me no one else could.

His hand moved up my body and he squeezed my breasts. I groaned with delight. He opened his sleepy eyes, smiled and looked at me and said "I missed you."

"I missed you too, why are you home?"

He shushed me and kissed me instead. I closed my eyes and kissed him back. His skin felt so warm against mine. He kissed my lips and my neck. He gave my ears a nibble, it tickled and I laughed. He ran his hands down my body. It ignited me and felt so good. He thrust himself inside of me and my body trembled. I groaned again. It was heaven. Our bodies intertwined and we climaxed together and then we just laid there as one.

I was starting to slowly drift back to sleep when he whispered,

"The wedding got called off. Celebrities – their lives are very different than yours and mine. You stay in bed; I'll get up with the munchkins." He kissed my forehead and crawled out of bed. I laid there in bed with a huge smile on my face, knowing that I didn't need to get up felt so nice, it didn't take long for me to fall back asleep.

When I finally woke up I looked at the clock and it was 1:00 in the afternoon. I couldn't remember the last time that I had slept in that late. I felt so good and I was so thankful to sleep as long as my body needed.

I listened and the house was quiet. No screaming or running. Silence.

I got myself ready and went downstairs and there was a note on the table:

> *The boys were excited to see dad so we went for a little adventure. Enjoy your time alone. Open the box. Just Relax. Love you ass-breath*

I laughed. It takes a special woman to take the word ass-breath as a term of endearment. I saw a little box on the table and opened it up. Inside was a beautiful bracelet. I usually opt for something simple but this one was gorgeous. Not gaudy but had some bling to it. He had put some serious thought into this one. I smiled. I had the day to myself.

I made myself a tea and grabbed my notebook from last night to help me to decide what to tackle today. I checked my phone and Stacey had called me 17 times. Time to get to work.

Chapter Ten

I FLIPPED THROUGH my notebook and then remembered about my late night email. It sparked my curiosity again and I sat down at the computer and opened up my email.

Dear Evy,

I have become a recent fan of your work and the great things you are doing for moms. It's by far the toughest job out the and I commend you on keeping it real. You are an inspiration to others in the journey of motherhood. I would like the opportunity to chat with you about your life as a mom, writer, entrepreneur and life coach – as this is what you have become to your fans. If you can please let me know if you would agree to let us be a

*gateway to helping more mothers, I
believe great things can happen for you.*

Most Sincerely,

Dee Parker

I sat there stunned. Dee Parker was a famous
talk show host and had a giant following and
she had just commended me on my work. She
had called me an inspiration. The woman who
was worth close to a billion dollars, knew who I
was, what I was about and wanted to talk to me.

I read it over 3 more times. I googled the email
address and it all looked legit. I couldn't hold it
in, I screamed out loud and then started crying,
happy tears. I was jumping around the room
when I felt my phone vibrating on the desk.

I saw it was Stacey calling. It brought me back
down to earth. We had to get a gameplan
together.

"Hi Stacey, what's happening?" as I held in a
laugh.

"Not much, same old. Except I'm freaking out.
There are so many t-shirts to make, box and
ship. Where have you been? I've been getting it

all organized this morning but I need production help big time. I call the girls and we're meeting at Chloe's house later ok?"

"Of course, Mark came home last night. I had no idea he was coming home so he can watch the kids and I am there for however long you need me to be there."

"Ha, how was the welcome home sex?" and she laughed.

I burst out laughing, "Sooooo nice, and then he got up with the boys and took them out. I got to sleep in and didn't have to take care of anyone.

"Ugh, I'm jealous, ok I'll let you enjoy your quiet time, I know how rare it is to get time to yourself. I'll see you later ok. Have fun, love you."

"Love you too." We hung up the phone. I didn't want to tell her about my email just yet. I wanted to see where this was going to go before I started sharing the news.

I again sat back down at my desk and re-read the email one last time then I clicked reply.

I watched the curser blink, blink, blink. What to say…?

Then as I always did, I just winged it, I found that was always the best way for the right words to come out. The longer I thought about it the less it would be sincere and I really wanted this to be as real as possible. After all, all of my articles I wrote were written in the same fashion.

Dear Dee,

I cannot express how inspiring it is to hear such kind words from such an amazing woman like yourself. Nothing in the world would make me happier than to speak with you (aside from a clean house and dinner that I didn't have to contribute to.) Please let me know when would work best with your schedule, as I'm sure you have one or two things on the go, and I will make it work on my end. Again, thank you so much and I really look forward to chatting with you.

Sending you my best wishes for a wonderful day. Evy

I hoped she had a good sense of humour and I clicked send. That was that, this crazy surprise of a lifetime was now in cyberspace.

***

I jumped over to the site to see check the action when I heard the bing of a new email alert. My curiosity wouldn't let me wait and I had to see if it was a reply from Dee. I laughed, definitely not but if I wanted Viagra delivered to my home – that could be arranged. There was no way she would respond back that fast. I shook it off and went back to the site. The traffic was picking up even more, sometimes I just liked to look at all the numbers and see the graphs and charts that monitor the sites growth. I set the graph from day one til today and it made me so proud to see it incline. I had over 100,000 active visitors on the site. I was humbled by the support and was so giddy about Dee and this giant order boom we experienced. Then I heard the bing of an email arriving.

I gave it a quick look and my heart stopped. It was a reply back from Dee Parker. I couldn't open it on my own. This was too big and exciting. But I needed to know what it said – it could just be an auto-reply. I felt like the fate of my life depended on this moment.

I stared at the computer. I couldn't do this alone, I needed someone to experience this with me. I sent Mark a quick text;

CAN YOU CALL ME WHEN YOU GET A CHANCE? IT'S TRULY IMPORTANT

His response came quickly

TRULY?? LOL GIVE ME 5 MIN

I was on pins an needles. My curiosity was killing me. Then the phone rang.

"What's up honey? You are supposed to be taking a break from us today, I know we are the center of your world and all but…"

I cut him off, "Shut up this is serious," I said.

He was quiet so I continued, "I got an email today from Dee Parker, do you know who she is? She's a huge deal. She said she was a fan of mine and wanted to meet me for an interview. Do you understand how crazy this is? So I wrote her back and she replied, SHE REPLIED!!!!" I was having trouble containing myself. "And she wrote back already, but I haven't read the email, should I read it now? I wanted you to be here and the girls, but I want to read it first to know if its good news but I want everyone to read it with me if it is…. ahhhhh I'm freaking out."

Mark started laughing. "Breath honey, I do know who Dee Parker is, she's a very sweet lady. I'm surprised she got in contact with you so soon."

"What?"

"I met her on the shoot I was on, we chatted one day. I told her what you did and how much your life had changed since you started this site, I filled her in on your journey and how you were helping other moms and she really seemed interested. I thought she was just being polite when she asked for your info. She really is a cool lady."

"You met her, and you told her about me? You did this?"

"No honey, you did this. I am so proud of you and I shared that pride with her."

My eyes welled up with happy tears.

"Ok that settles it, I'm going to read it right now. Are you ready?"

He laughed again, "ready when you are."

I sat at the computer, took a deep breath and click on the email. I read it aloud:

> *"Hi Evy, you are a genuine sweetheart. I am free next Wednesday at 4pm. If you are free then, I would love to meet you for dinner and meet your family as well so if I can intrude on your home, I'll bring the food.*
>
> *Cheers Dee*

"OMG, Mark she wants to come here!!! To our home." And I screamed and danced and cried. I forgot for a moment Mark was on the phone listening to my freak-out.

"Sorry, this is crazy, so crazy, what do I do?"

"Write her back and say dinner would be wonderful and pencil it into the calendar. I am so proud of you honey. This is huge and you did it. Now send the email stop working and get over here. I'm at Chloe and Adam's house right now and she's in cleaning mode and Adam and I want out of here."

So I wrote the reply back to her and again she replied back quickly with a confirmation. This was honestly the best day ever; I could not wait to tell my girls the news. I pack an overnight bag and headed over to Chloe's house.

Chapter Eleven

WHEN I ARRIVED at her house I rang the bell and knew my boys were still there. I could hear the herd of elephant's charge towards the door. It swung open.

"Mom, Dad's home!!!" Luke screamed at me as he came running at me and gave me a giant hug.

"I know sweetie, how was your day?" I asked.

"It was awesome. Dad took us swimming, then out for lunch, then we went visiting and tonight we're having a movie night and sleepover with my friends…This is the best day ever!!!!!!"

I looked behind Luke and I saw Mark and he was holding a sleeping toddler in each arm. He looked exhausted.

"I think I was a little too ambitious. But the boys had a blast. I don't know how you did it honey; you are a superhero."

He kissed me and smiled. "I'm going to take the crew home, you girls have fun, keep me posted on your news."

"I will, thank you for this, for everything."

"You deserve it, you are amazing." I kissed all the boys and waved good-bye.

Now it was time for girl's craft night!!

***

I walked into the house and found Chloe in the kitchen. She smiled, "Look, I'm finally losing the baby weight."

"You're a nut." I said and hugged her. I could feel the bones through her skin.

I have something special for you and I handed her a gift box.

She eyed it and gave me a quizzical look, she unwrapped everything and she was in tears laughing as she pulled everything out, along with her "medicine", I had stopped on the way over and bought rolling papers and a lighter. I also packed some chips and dip knowing that we might get the munchies.

"Come on, let's light one up so I can get the munchies and maybe eat some food. The girls should be here any minute. Let's do it the old school way and roll a big, fat joint." She laughed so hard, "who would have thought I would ever be the one to say that. That should get us all in the zone for what's lying ahead for us."

I sat down and started rolling one up. It had been such a long time since I had done this but all the little tricks came back to me.

It took me a little bit to get it all ready and by the time I did the doorbell rang and the girls had arrived. They had a feast of snacks with them and boxes of supplies for the shirts.

"I guess we all prepared for the munchies." I said and laughed as we showed them what we were up to. The ladies were both on board.

We sat in Chloe's living room. Her beautifully decorated and meticulously clean living room, "Are you sure you want to do this in here…It's going to be smelly…"

"Light it up." Was her response, "life is definitely too short to give a shit about that stuff now."

I lit it up and she took the very first hit. She breathed it in slow and leaned her head back. Let out a giant puff of smoke, laughed then coughed.

She passed it around and we all took a turn. It didn't take long for the giggles to kick in. It only took one of us to crack up before we spent the next 5 minutes laughing and not having any idea why.

"Thank you guys, for doing this with me. I am going to miss you guys when I'm gone, but I've made a vow that I am going to haunt each and every one of you for as long as it takes me to get into heaven. And when I get there safe and sound I'll let you know somehow. Like a random yellow rose that starts growing overnight in your garden. Something weird and spooky like that."

"We are going to miss you more…and if you want to give us a sign, send us winning lottery numbers, now that would be awesome."

She laughed, "I'll see what I can do, anyone else getting hungry? I think the munchies have officially kicked in and I haven't eaten anything in awhile. I've tried believe me."

We went into the kitchen and sat around her kitchen island. We dished out all of the food and snacks we had brought prepared our munchie feast.

When we had finished munching out we went back to the living room, opened all the windows and went over the gameplan. Stacey had cut all the designs to they need to be applied to the shirts, but first the shirts needed to be ironed, the decorated, boxed up and labelled. We each took a station and went to it. While we were working we started chatting about life and then I remembered I hadn't told them about the emails from Dee.

"So ladies, it seems we have our first major breakthrough. I got an email today from Dee Parker." They all stopped and stared at me, they knew this was serious business. "She's a fan and she wants to meet me and the family. Mark met her in Hawaii and they talked about the site and she was really intrigued, so she reached out. She's coming by next Wednesday at 4pm. Please tell me you'll all come." They were quiet, then there was nothing but screaming. They made me read the emails over and over to get the full effect. Then we hit that moment of total quiet. We were all lost in our own thoughts with huge smiles on our faces.

"I think Evy, as much as we want to be there with you. You should do this on your own. This is your brainchild. We just helped. This moment belongs to you." Leslie said.

"But all of you helped to get it where it is today." I replied.

"We know, but really, you deserve this." Stacey said.

We kept talking about what I would wear and say to Dee. It was exciting. Then we got back into the rhythm of our production line. We were making good progress but we still had a way to go. When we had about 25 orders left to go, I felt my eyes getting droopy and I couldn't fight the tiredness anymore. I sat on the couch and it felt like I was melting into it. It was so cozy and warm and before I knew if I was zonked out.

 It was an hour later when I woke up. My eyes felt dry and my mouth was like a dessert. I literally felt like I had to peel my tongue off the roof of my mouth.

I stood up, my head was spinning and I walked to the kitchen for water. Pasties. Chloe was in there already, "Do you have the pasties too?" she asked.

"Ugh I feel horrible," she said, "Do me a favour ok, honestly and truly, I think this interview is amazing, I think it's going to make you famous. Use this opportunity to your total advantage. Make a million dollars, please...be successful, don't forget about me..." and she started to cry,

"I am so scared, my daughter is going to grow up without me, she won't know me, Adam will remarry, I'll haunt them too, but he deserves happiness and one day I will only be a distant memory to them all…"

I hugged her and whispered to her,

"You will always have a place in their hearts, you made her, she will always love you and know that she was loved, even if you are not here with her on earth, she will know you. I promise you, I will make sure that happens."

"Thank you Evy, shhh don't tell the girls but you are my favourite. I love you so much."

"I love you too, come on, let's go to bed."

I tucked her into bed and then crawled in beside her. I sent Mark a text to say goodnight and he replied back pretty quickly with an I love you, then a few moments later he texted – Adam says to give Chloe a kiss from him and say he'd see her in the morning. I gently kissed her cheek and whispered in her ear, "that was from

Adam, he says he loves you and he'll see you in the morning." I texted back "done".

Chloe was drifting into a deep sleep and replied, "just incase, give him a kiss back for me…" she closed her eyes and that night she fell into her eternal sleep. She passed away peacefully in her sleep.

Chapter Twelve

I WOKE UP in the middle of the night and took a moment to figure out where I was, when I got my bearings I rolled over and listened for the sound of Chloe breathing. I didn't hear anything. I gently nudged her, nothing, I knew…at this very moment, my dear friend was gone. I rolled her over and her limp, lifeless body turned. I felt a weird sense of calmness, I kissed her cold forehead and went downstairs to tell Stacey and Leslie. They were both still in the living room, they had fallen asleep on the other set of couches. The finished pile of boxes surrounded them.. I woke them both, they were groggy.

"Girls, Chloe is gone." I said.

"Where did she go?" Leslie asked still half asleep.

"On her way to heaven…"

This woke them both up immediately. "What???"

"Chloe passed away, she is upstairs…" and I broke down, and so did they and we cried together.

"I'll call an ambulance." Stacey said, "Oh god, who's going to call Adam?"

"He's at our house, I'll call…"

I dialed Mark's number first, he answered on the fourth ring,

"Hello," he said in a groggy voice, "miss me already??"

"Mark, is Adam in the same room as you right now?"

"What time is it? No, he's sleeping downstairs, why?"

"It's Chloe, she died, in her sleep, Stacey is calling an ambulance right now."

"Fuck…." And then there was silence, "do you want me to tell him?"

"It would be best for him to hear it from a friend, but keep me on the phone ok, just incase…"

"fuck, fuck, fuck, ok…hold on."

I heard him open the door and down the stairs. This was the longest walk ever, but I knew Mark was probably taking his time too, how do you tell someone their wife died…I guess I was about to find out. I heard another door open and snoring, then a thump, was that a pillow?

"Adam, dude?"

A giant groan, "what???"

"I need to tell you something…Evy is on the phone…"

"Chloe died right?"

There was a pause, "yes, man, I'm sorry."

"I was just dreaming about her, there were yellow roses and we were in a giant meadow together. I knew it, is Evy on the phone?"

"Yes, here" and I heard the phone being passed.

"Evy?"

"Yes, Adam, I am so sorry…"

"Did you kiss her goodnight for me?"

I smiled, "I did, and she said for me to give you a kiss back, just incase…"

"Thank you, I'm grateful she had you with her. I'm going drive home right now ok."

"Ok, Stacey has called an ambulance but I'll tell them to wait until you get here…"

And we hung up.

Chapter Thirteen

WE FRANTICALLY WENT around the house and made sure there were no signs of our "girl's night" left hanging around, but most of the smell had dissipated anyway.

We were silent when the ambulance arrived. They went through their routine but the paramedics knew that she had passed on. They carefully lifted her body onto the stretcher. The wheeled her into the ambulance.

I asked them to please wait til her husband arrived. I knew that he would want to go with her. They agreed to wait five minutes but then they had to leave. Adam arrived with 20 seconds to spare. We all hugged him and he climbed into the back of the ambulance for what would be the last trip he would take with his wife.

***

Once they were gone the girls and I went back inside the house. It seemed so inappropriate to be in her home knowing that now she wasn't here with us. Stacey went into the kitchen and starting making coffee. Leslie and I began cleaning up the house. We had left it a mess of papers, tape and boxes.

When the smell of coffee filled the house we took a break from cleaning and we all took a spot at the kitchen island. We took a few sips and then Leslie broke the silence.

"What do we do now? I mean we can only tidy up for so long..." she wiped away a lone tear from her cheek.

"I know it sounds horrible, but I'm tired...can we try to sleep...just a bit..." Stacey said. "The kids have been driving me crazy and I really was looking forward to getting some sleep…ugh, am I really that horrible of a person to say that right now?"

We looked at her and smiled.

"No, we all need sleep, we know coffee doesn't work as well as it used to…why don't we all try to take a quick nap, come on." I grabbed their hands and we went upstairs into Chloe's bedroom. We all laid down in her bed, none of us brave enough to sleep in the spot she had passed away in. That spot we kept for her, the three of us all curled up together and wept and slept.

***

I don't know what time it was when we fell asleep or how long we actually slept for. I felt sad and yet relieved that my dear friend had found peace and her suffering had ended.

I was woken up by the vibration of my phone in my pocket. I looked at the number – Mark had messaged me and said he was on his way over with Adam and the kids. I looked at the time and it was after 10:00am. I looked over at the girls, they were passed out cold still. We were all clearly in need of sleep.

I brushed my teeth and got dressed then I tiptoed downstairs. I looked around the house, of all the smiling pictures of Chloe's beautiful face.

I heard the front door open and turned to see Adam, Mark and the kids. The guys were holding back tears and Lexi looked pretty somber.

"What would you like us to do?" I asked Adam.

He sent all the kids outside into the yard to play and we sat down at the table.

"You know Chloe, she planned everything. A few weeks ago she gave me a portfolio of everything she wanted," he started to laugh, "man she was such a control freak…"

We smiled and chatted about the service and shared funny stories. Halfway through Stacey and Leslie came down and joined us.

Adam had told Lexi that her mom had turned into an angel during the night. They had been preparing her for what was going to happen so while she was sad she felt better knowing their mom was now an angel in heaven that would watch over her always.

***

Three days later the service for Chloe was held. It was simple but beautiful. She had requested nothing lavish – she did not want it to be a sad event but a celebration of life. We told jokes and shared funny stories and cried both happy and sad tears. We had all decided to use yellow roses to celebrate her life.

My heart felt so heavy – here was a woman who gave always to others, and being with her in her final moments on earth made me feel so grateful that I was there with her, and yet I felt so sad that it wasn't Adam that was there with her instead.

I remember looking over at him during the service and I could see him struggling to keep the tears back. He loved her so deeply. And her daughter, so young to lose their beautiful mom. How were they going to cope without her, what did the future hold for them? My heart was breaking for them. She was gone forever. And I let the tears flow.

Chapter Fourteen

4 days later

WE WERE ALL doing our best to get back to some sort of normal. I made sure that Mark kept in touch with Adam to make sure he was doing ok and I was getting things ready for the dinner date with Dee. So much had happened and I still had bouts of sadness when I thought about everything that had happened.

I thought about cancelling but this was a once in lifetime opportunity and Chloe would be mad if I cancelled. I was nervous and excited. I had tidied up the house and made everyone promise to be on their best behaviour. Leslie and Stacey called and wished me good luck and made me promise to call them as soon as it was over.

I was sweating so bad my armpits were like mini-pools. I changed my shirt three times before I saw her entourage arrive. There was no escaping it. This was it. Then right on cue, Ben pooped his pants, Tom started crying and Luke began running around the house singing at the top of his lungs. I looked at Mark and without having to say a word he grabbed both babies in his arms and brought them upstairs. Not bad only one crazy child and a poop smell in the air. What a perfect way to welcome a celebrity into our home.

The doorbell rang and Lance barked like crazy. I didn't even think to put him outside. He bolted to the door and Luke chased after him screaming. I said a small prayer, "Dear Lord, please grant me peace, and let my family not be savages. Amen."

I opened the door and saw 2 bodyguards and assistant, a photographer and a cameraman. Bringing up the rear was Dee, she smiled. She looked perfect and then as Lance ran outside he jumped up on her. She gave him a pat on the head and a quick scratch. Then she looked up and smiled.

"Hello, you must be Evy," and she extended her hand to me. "Please excuse all this fuss, this crew is constantly around looking for any opportunity to document my life. You'll get used to it." And then she looked at Luke, "and you must be Evy's husband Mark?" Luke looked at her and smiled, "No way, I'm Luke, Dad is upstairs because Ben pooped his pants and Tom is crying and mom was losing her marbles."

Dee laughed and walked inside with her crew. Here went nothing.

***

I showed Dee around the house and all I could smell was poop, what did that child eat I wondered. Dee and I sat on the couch and had some small chit chat when I heard Mark yell from upstairs, "Evy, watch out..." and then I heard the thumping of Ben sliding down the stairs. I looked up and there he was running naked towards Dee. He was laughing so hard as he streaked past me, I took a quick glance at his bum and was thankful it was cleaned.

"Well, hello handsome," she said as he hugged her. He looked at her and pointed to him bum, "Big stinky poop bum all clean."

I could see she was trying to hold it in and then she just burst out laughing. She looked at me, "Is everyday like this?" she asked.

"Pretty much," I answered as I scooped Ben up and passed him back to Mark who had now made his way downstairs.

He waved, "Hi Dee, good to see you again, welcome to the chaos. I'll be back down in a minute once I can wrestle some clothes on this monkey." He threw Ben over his shoulder and went back upstairs.

"So Evy, tell me about this site that you've developed, why and how did it all come about?"

Her camera crew moved in closer.

"Well, I had hit a low point in my life and I was vs where I thought I would be were in very different directions. I was having a really hard time accepting this and motherhood was a lot harder than I anticipated. I felt very alone and confused and tired. I honestly thought about ending my life. That's how low I was…"

"And what made you decide not to?"

"Luke came into the bathroom, and we sat together, and he saw how sad mom was. Being with him at that moment made me not want him to see me like this. I had to step up and become a strong mom for him, for my boys. Mark and I were also at a crossroads. We had an honest and real conversation and decided that we were going to survive this together. This inspired me to build the site to give inspiration to all the moms out there that are struggling. Let them know they are not alone and that they are all doing an amazing job. Even on the days they may not feel like it."

"So what did you do before kids, what were your goals?"

"Before I worked for a magazine. I wanted to travel and meet celebrities. I had made my way to head writer in a few short years and then I met Mark, and we got married and then kids came along and I had to choose between the job or the family."

"What if you could do both?"

I laughed, "I would love to know how that's possible."

"Everything is possible; it just depends on how much of yourself you can put into it. Have you done any work with television?"

"I've dabbled in tv but I've been out of the game for awhile now."

"But it will come back to you right?"

I paused, "Why...?"

"Because I would love to have someone like you on my team, someone who had been there, changed focus and came out ahead. Look at what you have done. You have a huge following and people trust and love you. I can use that energy and creative mind of yours."

"But what would I do?"

"Pitch ideas, write segments, source out guests and sponsors. You would be my main go-to girl."

I was speechless, "I…what?"

And finally Mark came downstairs with a clothed Ben.

"Think about it, come on, let's have some pizza for dinner, I thought that would be a safe choise." With a wave of her hand her assistant out of no where brought 6 boxes of pizza into the kitchen.

"Think about what?" Mark asked.

"Dee wants me to work for her, as her go-to girl for the show." I said.

Mark raised his eyebrow at me and said, "How long was I upstairs?"

***

We sat around the table and divided out the pizza as we continued talking.

"I just think Evy is so well-suited for this, look what she has accomplished in such a short period of time. Of course working for me will take up quite a bit of your time so you site may have to get scaled back, and you'll need a nanny for the boys, but I can help with that."

It was now my turn to raise my eyebrow, as much as I admired this woman, who was she to start planning my life?

"It's a lot to think about and it's not something that I can answer you on today that's for sure, there is a lot to consider."

"What's there to consider? Come work for me, you can hire a few people to manage your site, contract out your shop overseas, you'll pay much smaller margins that way on product."

"It's not just about money, it's about giving back and helping fellow moms. That's the whole point. I don't think I can give it up."

Then it went quiet, I don't think Dee was used to hearing people stand up to her but this was my life and I couldn't allow someone else to call the shots.

"Well, ok then, think it over, you know how to get in touch with me. I'm sorry to say that I must run, more people to meet today. It truly was a pleasure meeting you and your family, you are very blessed and I now see why you are where you are in your life." She hugged me and gave the boys a big hug too, she shook Mark's hand

and just like that she was gone. Her crew cleaned up the last of the pizza and they were gone too.

I looked at Mark, "Was it something I said?"

He hugged me, "You sweetie, just stood your ground against one of the most powerful and influential woman of our time – yes I think it was something you said. And I couldn't be more proud of you."

"You understand where I'm coming from right? I can't just quit my work now, there are so many people depending on me."

"I know,"

"But it is an opportunity to work for such an amazing person."

"Doing what again?" he asked.

"I would be in charge of finding guests, promo materials, meeting sponsors…"

"And when do you think this all takes place?"

"All times of the day, and night, and weekends…so I would always be working…"

"And what you have going now…what do you like about that?"

"The freedom to work when I want, and how I can work around our life and be around the boys and that it's all mine, well, mine and the girls."

"What is your heart and your gut telling you?"

"Ugh, to say thanks but no thanks and keep doing what I'm doing….ahhhhh that's crazy to pass up this opportunity though."

"This will not be the only opportunity; this is just the beginning."

Go take some time and write her a letter. Speak from the heart. Talk to the girls too.

***

I called Leslie. I knew Stacey was at her house and she put me on speaker phone.

They were squealing with excitement.

"So, fill us in. What happened?"

I gave them the rundown from start to finish and they agreed with my decision to keep doing what we have created. I think they felt a sense of relief to hear how important this was to me too. They gave me the courage to write this email;

Dear Dee,

Thank you for taking the time to come and meet with me and my family today. It was such a special thing to have you in my home. I was shocked when you offered me a position to come and work for you, however, regretfully I have to decline. While I know it is an amazing opportunity I cannot give up on what I have started. The changes I am making in other people's lives is too important to stop now and think only of myself and my needs.

I hope you understand

Thank you

Evy

I clicked send. Short and sweet, the best way to do it.

I turned the computer off and went upstairs to hang out with all my boys. We turned on a movie and all cuddled on the couch. It felt nice to have them all so close to me. Then I felt the vibration of one of them laughing, then I caught the whiff of fart.

"Seriously, you guys are so gross." They all burst out laughing.

After we tucked the kids into bed I told Mark that I needed some quiet time. He understood and I went to reflect on what had happened that day. I felt good about my decision to decline Dee's offer.

I got lost in my thoughts, I kept re-running the conversation I had with Dee through my mind. Now the other side of my brain kicked in. Did I make the right choice? All through my schooling and into my career this was the opportunity that I always wanted. I mean this did not happen everyday. An opportunity to work with one of the most famous women in television and I passed on it.

Then the other side of my brain stepped in and reminded me that my life was different than when those goals were made. And I was successful in my own right.

I was having this on-going battle inside. I checked my emails I still hadn't gotten a response from Dee but I did see something impossible and email that came from Chloe's email. Obviously she didn't send it, I clicked on it,

> Hi Evy, this is going to seem weird but Chloe asked me to forward you this email in the event of her passing. Like I said, she was prepared for everything. Take Care, Adam

> Dearest Evy,

> I knew I would haunt you from beyond the grave. I know you are missing me so much but do try to move on. If you are reading this, it means that I didn't get a chance to sit down with you to talk business. It makes me sad that I wasn't able to share this news with you in person but I was waiting on a huge milestone

before I could share with you how amazing you are.

I know you thought that your main revenue was just starting with the sale of merchandise, which yes it did bring in a good amount of money, however your other income that is bringing in quite a bit of cash are the ads you sell on your site and your affiliate links. You can thank Stacey, Leslie and I for this. You are an amazing writer and creative person but you stink at adverting and sales. Thankfully you had me who believed in you every step of the way. Please follow this link and enter the following user name and password. I love you my dear friend. xoxo Chloe

WTF. Chloe had been making me money without me even knowing about it. I was shocked. How did I not know about this? What did she mean about a huge milestone? I clicked on the link which took me to an investment website and entered her information she provided. After some searching I came across a link to "see your account balance" I clicked on it and my eyes and my brain had a disconnect as to what they were seeing and understanding.

Your current account balance

$973, 562.53

I just stared. That rascal was stock-piling money to get me to a million dollars. How one earth did she do this? So delved deeper and it was all legit. She was making me money all over the site, affiliate links, ad links, ad sales. They had made us almost a million without me even knowing. She never said a word. I knew what she was planning though. Once it hit the one million mark she would simply hand it over and say something like "see how easy it is to save?"

Well, if I needed a sign that I had made the right decision this was it. Then as if it was planned, my email dinged and it was from Dee.

> *Hi Evy, I knew it would be a long-shot trying to get you to come work for me since you have become so successful on your own. If life has taught me anything it's that you have to take chances and go*

outside of you comfort zone. The results are always so much better.

If you are free on Thursday, November 19th I would love to have you and the family fly up to see me (all expenses paid of course) and nothing would make me more proud to have you as a guest on my show.

Let's share with the world how amazing you really are. Sound good?

Dee

I replied

Yes, that sounds really good. Let's do it.

I clicked send and I cried. The happiest tears.

I sat for a few more minutes and gained my composure. I went upstairs to find Mark. All the lights were off so I knew he had gone to bed. I snuck into the bedroom and snuggled up to him. He reached out and grabbed my arm and wrapped it around him. He mumbles, "So, do you feel better about your decision now."

"Yes, Can I ask you a question? When I was at my lowest, did you give up on me? Did you want to call it quits?"

He rolled over, "I never have nor will I ever give up on you. I just didn't know how to motivate you. But you did it on your own, I was worried you were going to leave me, did you know that. We're past it and I love you and no matter what happens I will support you. I think what you are doing is amazing, you are honestly making a difference in other people's lives. Not many people can say that. You can."

I kissed him, "thank you, do you want to hear something amazing..." I tried to keep my excitement in check, "we are almost millionaires and Dee wants me to be a guest on her show."

He sat straight up in bed, "WHAT?? What happened when you went downstairs?"

"Chloe and the girls had been making money through the site. I had no idea, but now I do, and when I was down there Dee messaged me and asked me to be a guest on her show, she wants to fly us in."

He turned on the lamp by the bed, and he looked at me, I have never been so proud to call you my wife." He kissed me and hugged me and kept muttering "a million dollars, one million dollars, I can't believe it. How..." then laughter. We laid in bed saying this over and over and laughing with excitement.

What a way life had come in a year. From rock bottom to sitting on top of the world. It goes to show never give up and follow your heart. The universe will guide us but we need to be willing to listen.

Epilogue

Thursday, November 19th

I WAS STANDING backstage waiting to get my cue to enter on stage to Dee's show. Mark and Luke were sitting in the audience and the younger boys were with Dee's assistant watching from the green room.

The music cued, I heard the audience clapping as my name was announced. I walked out and waved and smiled as I made my way towards Dee.

She introduced me to the crowd and began asking me series of questions, many were the ones she had asked when she visited our home. "When did I begin the site?", "What was my inspiration?", "Who helps me with it?" Then she hit me with the big one,

"You suffered a great loss this year, one of your original girls as I understand, can you tell me what happened?"

"Chloe was one of the backbones of the site, but also one of the most amazing women I have ever known. She was diagnosed with cancer and it was so aggressive..." I was getting choked up, "She just didn't have enough time...She was taken far too soon. It's because of her we designed this new piece, as a tribute to her." I pointed to my shirt, it was white with a yellow rose that had petals the looked like an angel. "It turned out to be our biggest seller to date. It was our tribute to Chloe. With the proceeds from these shirts we have started the Chloe Edwards Foundation to assist with families affected by cancer, as well, we have started a trust fund for her daughter..."and then the tears started. Dang it.

Dee held my hand and offered me a tissue, she whispered to me, ignoring the audience, "I am so sorry for your loss, I know she must have been so special to you. I think this is a wonderful tribute to her and her family."

I looked up, "Thank you."

Then she spoke to the audience, "I feel so inspired by you Evy for everything you are doing, you are making a difference in many people's lives, I would like to make a contribution to Chloe's Foundation, then she whipped out a giant cheque for $25,000. I think this will help." The audience cheered and I was stunned. Then she continued talking, "and I would also like to give you something as well. You have come a far way and your journey should be celebrated as well. For you Evy," and she pulled out another giant cheque in the amount of $25,000, "this is for you and your family."

I looked at her, then at Mark and I hugged her so hard, "thank you so much, this is amazing...then the audience broke out in hysterical laughter.

I turned and saw not one but two of my children, running across the stage. Dee's assistant was following after them, she yelled to me as she ran by, "They tricked me, they planned it, they were there one second and gone the next…I'm so sorry."

I looked at Dee and she was laughing hysterically, her audience was laughing even harder. I caught Mark's eye and he shrugged. He knew that chasing them was exactly what they wanted.

Dee was wiping tears from her eyes she was laughing so hard.

"That was by far the best ending we have ever had on our show." Dee said through giggles.

I smiled, even though we had now reached the million-dollar mark in the bank, I was on tv with one of the most famous women in the world my kids were still the same and I wouldn't change a thing.

Life was good.

About the Author

Sarah Lawrence is a full-time mom to three busy but amazing boys. When she's not covered in dirt from playing in the mud, she finds peace in her writing. She also chronicles her mom-life on Facebook and twitter.

Get in Touch

Email: fromsarahtonin@outlook.com

Like us on: facebook.com/fromsarahtonin

Twitter @fromsarahtonin